Auguste Groner

The Case of the Pocket Diary found in the Snow

Leseklassiker

Auguste Groner

The Case of the Pocket Diary found in the Snow

ISBN/EAN: 9783955630294

Auflage: 1

Erscheinungsjahr: 2013

Erscheinungsort: Bremen, Deutschland

Leseklassiker

Contents

INTRODUCTION TO JOE MULLER

Joseph Muller, Secret Service detective of the Imperial Austrian police, is one of the great experts in his profession. In personality he differs greatly from other famous detectives. He has neither the impressive authority of Sherlock Holmes, nor the keen brilliancy of Monsieur Lecoq. Muller is a small, slight, plain-looking man, of indefinite age, and of much humbleness of mien. A naturally retiring, modest disposition, and two external causes are the reasons for Muller's humbleness of manner, which is his chief characteristic. One cause is the fact that in early youth a miscarriage of justice gave him several years in prison, an experience which cast a stigma on his name and which made it impossible for him, for many years after, to obtain honest employment. But the world is richer, and safer, by Muller's early misfortune. For it was this experience which threw him back on his own peculiar talents for a livelihood, and drove him into the police force. Had he been able to enter any other profession, his genius might have been stunted to a mere pastime, instead of being, as now, utilised for the public good.

Then, the red tape and bureaucratic etiquette which attaches to every governmental department, puts the secret service men of the Imperial police on a par with the lower ranks of the subordinates. Muller's official rank is scarcely much higher than that of a policeman, although kings and councillors consult him and the Police Department realises to the full what a treasure it has in him. But official red tape, and his early misfortune... prevent the giving of any higher official standing to even such a genius. Born and bred to such conditions, Muller understands them, and his natural modesty of disposition asks for no outward honours, asks for nothing but an income sufficient for his simple needs, and for aid and opportunity to occupy himself in the way he most enjoys.

Joseph Muller's character is a strange mixture. The kindest-hearted man in the world, he is a human bloodhound when once the lure of the trail has caught him. He scarcely eats or sleeps when the chase is on, he does not seem to know human weakness nor fatigue, in spite of his frail body. Once put on a case his mind delves and delves until it finds a clue, then something awakes within him, a spirit akin to that which holds the bloodhound nose to trail, and he will accomplish the apparently impossible, he will track down his victim when the entire machinery of a great police department seems helpless to discover anything. The high chiefs and commissioners grant a condescending permission when Muller asks, "May I do this? ... or may I handle this case this way?" both parties knowing all the while that it is a farce, and that the department waits helpless until this humble little man saves its honour by solving some problem before which its intricate machinery has stood dazed and puzzled.

This call of the trail is something that is stronger than anything else in Muller's mentality, and now and then it brings him into conflict with the department,... or with his own better nature. Sometimes his unerring instinct discovers secrets in high places, secrets which the Police Department is bidden to hush up and leave untouched. Muller is then taken off the case, and left idle for a while if he persists in his opinion as to the true facts. And at other times, Muller's own warm heart gets him into trouble. He will track down his victim, driven by the power in his soul which is stronger than all volition; but when he has this victim in the net, he will sometimes discover him to be a much finer, better man than the other individual, whose wrong at this particular criminal's hand set in motion the machinery of justice. Several times that has happened to Muller, and each time his heart got the better of his professional instincts, of his practical common-sense, too, perhaps,... at least as far as his own advancement was concerned, and he warned the victim, defeating his own work. This peculiarity of Muller's character caused his undoing at last, his official undoing that is, and compelled his retirement from the force. But his advice is often sought unofficially by the Department, and to those who know, Muller's hand can be seen in the unravelling of many a famous case.

The following stories are but a few of the

many interesting cases that have come within the experience of this great detective. But they give a fair portrayal of Muller's peculiar method of working, his looking on himself as merely an humble member of the Department, and the comedy of his acting under "official orders" when the Department is in reality following out his directions.

THE CASE OF THE POCKET DIARY FOUND IN THE SNOW

CHAPTER ONE.
THE DISCOVERY IN THE SNOW

A quiet winter evening had sunk down upon the great city. The clock in the old clumsy church steeple of the factory district had not yet struck eight, when the side door of one of the large buildings opened and a man came out into the silent street.

It was Ludwig Amster, one of the working-men in the factory, starting on his homeward way. It was not a pleasant road, this street along the edge of the city. The town showed itself from its most disagreeable side here, with malodorous factories, rickety tenements, untidy open stretches and dumping grounds offensive both to eye and nostril.

Even by day the street that Amster took was empty; by night it was absolutely quiet and dark, as dark as were the thoughts of the solitary man. He walked along, brooding over his troubles. Scarcely an hour before he had been discharged from the factory because of his refusal to submit to the injustice of his foreman.

The yellow light of the few lanterns show nothing but high board walls and snow drifts, stone heaps, and now and then the remains of a neglected garden. Here and there a stunted tree or a wild shrub bent their twigs under the white burden which the winter had laid upon them. Ludwig Amster, who had walked this street for several years, knew his path so well that he could take it blindfolded. The darkness did not worry him, but he walked somewhat more slowly than usual, for he knew that under the thin covering of fresh-fallen snow there lay the ice of the night before. He walked carefully, watching for the slippery places.

He had been walking about half an hour, perhaps, when he came to a cross street. Here he noticed the tracks of a wagon, the trace still quite fresh, as the slowly falling flakes did not yet cover it. The tracks led out towards the north, out on to the hilly, open fields.

Amster was somewhat astonished. It was very seldom that a carriage came into this neighbourhood, and yet these narrow wheel-tracks could have been made only by an equipage of that character. The heavy trucks which passed these roads occasionally had much wider wheels. But Amster was to find still more to astonish him.

In one corner near the cross-roads stood a solitary lamp-post. The light of the lamp fell sharply on the snow, on the wagon tracks, and — on something else besides.

Amster halted, bent down to look at it, and shook his head as if in doubt.

A number of small pieces of glass gleamed

up at him and between them, like tiny roses, red drops of blood shone on the white snow. All this was a few steps to one side of the wagon tracks.

"What can have happened here — here in this weird spot, where a cry for help would never be heard? where there would be no one to bring help?"

So Amster asked himself, but his discovery gave him no answer. His curiosity was aroused, however, and he wished to know more. He followed up the tracks and saw that the drops of blood led further on, although there was no more glass. The drops could still be seen for a yard further, reaching out almost to the board fence that edged the sidewalk. Through the broken planks of this fence the rough bare twigs of a thorn bush stretched their brown fingers. On the upper side of the few scattered leaves there was snow, and blood.

Amster's wide serious eyes soon found something else. Beside the bush there lay a tiny package. He lifted it up. It was a small, light, square package, wrapped in ordinary brown paper. Where the paper came together it was fastened by two little lumps of black bread, which were still moist. He turned the package over and shook his head again. On the other side was written, in pencil, the lettering uncertain, as if scribbled in great haste and in agitation, the sentence, "Please take this to the nearest police station."

The words were like a cry for help, frozen on to the ugly paper. Amster shivered; he had a feeling that this was a matter of life and death.

The wagon tracks in the lonely street, the broken pieces of glass and the drops of blood, showing that some occupant of the vehicle had broken the window, in the hope of escape, perhaps, or to throw out the package which should bring assistance — all these facts grouped themselves together in the brain of the intelligent working-man to form some terrible tragedy where his assistance, if given at once, might be of great use. He had a warm heart besides, a heart that reached out to this unknown who was in distress, and who threw out the call for help which had fallen into his hands.

He waited no longer to ponder over the matter, but started off at a full run for the nearest police station. He rushed into the room and told his story breathlessly.

They took him into the next room, the office of the commissioner for the day. The official in charge, who had been engaged in earnest conversation with a small, frail-looking, middle-aged man, turned to Amster with a question as to what brought him there.

"I found this package in the snow."

"Let me see it."

Amster laid it on the table. The older man

looked at it, and as the commissioner was about to open it, he handed him a paper-knife with the words: "You had better cut it open, sir."

"Why?"

"It is best not to injure the seals that fasten a package."

"Just as you say, Muller," answered the young commissioner, smiling. He was still very young to hold such an office, but then he was the son of a Cabinet Minister, and family connections had obtained this responsible position for him so soon. Kurt von Mayringen was his name, and he was a very good-looking young man, apparently a very good-natured young man also, for he took this advice from a subordinate with a most charming smile. He knew, however, that this quiet, pale-faced little man in the shabby clothes was greater than he, and that it was mere accident of birth that put him, Kurt von Mayringen, instead of Joseph Muller, in the position of superior.

The young commissioner had had most careful advice from headquarters as to Muller, and he treated the secret service detective, who was one of the most expert and best known men in the profession, with the greatest deference, for he knew that anything Muller might say could be only of value to him with his very slight knowledge of his business. He took the knife, therefore, and carefully cut open the paper, taking out a tiny little notebook, on the outer side of which a handsome monogram gleamed up at him in golden letters.

"A woman made this package," said Muller, who had been looking at the covering very carefully; "a blond woman."

The other two looked at him in astonishment. He showed them a single blond hair which had been in one of the bread seals.

"How I was murdered." Those were the words that Commissioner von Mayringen read aloud after he had hastily turned the first few pages of the notebook, and had come to a place where the writing was heavily underscored.

The commissioner and Amster were much astonished at these words, but the detective still gazed quietly at the seals of the wrapping.

"This heading reads like insanity," said the commissioner. Muller shrugged his shoulders, then turned to Amster. "Where did you find the package?"

"In Garden street."

"When?"

"About twenty minutes ago."

Amster gave a short and lucid account of his discovery. His intelligent face and well-chosen words showed that he had observation and the power to describe correctly what he had observed. His honest eyes inspired confidence.

"Where could they have been taking the woman?" asked the detective, more of himself than of the others.

The commissioner searched hastily through the notebook for a signature, but without success. "Why do you think it is a woman? This writing looks more like a man's hand to me. The letters are so heavy and — "

"That is only because they are written with broad pen," interrupted Muller, showing him the writing on the package; "here is the same hand, but it is written with a fine hard pencil, and you can see distinctly that this is a woman's handwriting. And besides, the skin on a man's thumb does not show the fine markings that you can see here on these bits of bread that have been used for seals."

The commissioner rose from his seat. "You may be right, Muller. We will take for granted, then, that there is a woman in trouble. It remains to be seen whether she is insane or not."

"Yes, that remains to be seen," said Muller dryly, as he reached for his overcoat.

"You are going before you read what is in the notebook?" asked Commissioner von Mayringen.

Muller nodded. "I want to see the wagon tracks before they are lost; it may help me to discover something else. You can read the book and make any arrangements you find necessary after that."

Muller was already wrapped in his overcoat. "Is it snowing now?" He turned to Arnster.

"Some flakes were falling as I came here."

"All right. Come with me and show me the way." Muller nodded carelessly to his superior officer, his mind evidently already engrossed in thoughts of the interesting case, and hurried out with Amster. The commissioner was quite satisfied with the state of affairs. He knew the case was in safe hands. He seated himself at his desk again and began to read the little book which had come into his hands so strangely. His eyes ran more and more rapidly over the closely written pages, as his interest grew and grew.

When, half an hour later, he had finished the reading, he paced restlessly up and down the room, trying to bring order into the thoughts that rushed through his brain. And one thought came again and again, and would not be denied in spite of many improbabilities, and many strange things with which the book was full; in spite, also, of the varying, uncertain handwriting and style of the message. This one thought was, "This woman is not insane."

While the young official was pondering over the problem, Muller entered as quietly as ever, bowed, put his hat and cane in their places, and shook the snow off his clothing. He was evidently pleased about something. Kurt von Mayringen did not notice his entrance. He was again at the desk with the open book before him, staring at the mysterious words, "How I was murdered."

"It is a woman, a lady of position. And if she is mad, then her madness certainly has method." Muller said these words in his usual quiet way, almost indifferently. The young commissioner started up and snatched for the fine white handkerchief which the detective handed him. A strong sweet perfume filled the room. "It is hers?" he murmured.

"It is hers," said Muller. "At least we can take that much for granted, for the handkerchief bears the same monogram, A. L., which is on the notebook."

Commissioner von Mayringen rose from his chair in evident excitement. "Well?" he asked.

It was a short question, but full of meaning, and one could see that he was waiting in great excitement for the answer. Muller reported what he had discovered. The commissioner thought it little enough, and shrugged his shoulders impatiently when the other had finished.

Muller noticed his chief's dissatisfaction and smiled at it. He himself was quite content with what he had found.

"Is that all?" murmured the commissioner, as if disappointed.

"That is all," repeated the detective calmly, and added, "That is a good deal. We have here a closely written notebook, the contents of which, judging by your excitement, are evidently important. We have also a handkerchief with an unusual perfume on it. I repeat that this is quite considerable. Besides this, we have the seals, and we know several other things. I believe that we can save this lady, of if it be too late, we can avenge her at least."

The commissioner looked at Muller in surprise. "We are in a city of more than a million inhabitants," he said, almost timidly.

"I have hunted criminals in two hemispheres, and I have found them," said Muller simply. The young commissioner smiled and held out his hand. "Ah, yes, Muller — I keep forgetting the great things you have done. You are so quiet about it."

"What I have done is only what any one could do who has that particular faculty. I do only what is in human power to do, and the cleverest criminal can do no more. Besides which, we all know that every criminal commits some stupidity, and leaves some trace behind him. If it is really a crime which we have found the trace of here, we will soon discover it." Muller's editorial "we" was a matter of formality. He might with more truth have used the singular pronoun.

"Very well, then, do what you can," said the

commissioner with a friendly smile.

The older man nodded, took the book and its wrappings from the desk, and went into a small adjoining room.

The commissioner sent for an attendant and gave him the order to fetch a pot of tea from a neighbouring saloon. When the tray arrived, he placed several good cigars upon it, and sent it in to Muller. Taking a cigar himself, the commissioner leaned back in his sofa corner to think over this first interesting case of his short professional experience. That it concerned a lady in distress made it all the more romantic.

In his little room the detective, put in good humour by the thoughtful attention of his chief, sat down to read the book carefully. While he studied its contents his mind went back over his search in the silent street outside.

He and Amster had hurried out into the raw chill of the night, reaching the spot of the first discovery in about ten or fifteen minutes. Muller found nothing new there. But he was able to discover in which direction the carriage had been going. The hoof marks of the single horse which had drawn it were still plainly to be seen in the snow.

"Will you follow these tracks in the direction from which they have come?" he asked of Amster. "Then meet me at the station and report what you have seen."

"Very well, sir," answered the workman. The two men parted with a hand shake.

Before Muller started on to follow up the tracks in the other direction, he took up one of the larger pieces' of glass. "Cheap glass," he said, looking at it carefully. "It was only a hired cab, therefore, and a one-horse cab at that."

He walked on slowly, following the marks of the wheels. His eyes searched the road from side to side, looking for any other signs that might have been left by the hand which had thrown the package out of the window. The snow, which had been falling softly thus far, began to come down in heavier flakes, and Muller quickened his pace. The tracks would soon be covered, but they could still be plainly seen. They led out into the open country, but when the first little hill had been climbed a drift heaped itself up, cutting off the trail completely.

Muller stood on the top of this knoll at a spot where the street divided. Towards the right it led down into a factory suburb; towards the left the road led on to a residence colony, and straight ahead the way was open, between fields, pastures and farms, over moors, to another town of considerable size lying beside a river. Muller knew all this, but his knowledge of the locality was of little avail, for all traces of the carriage wheels were lost.

He followed each one of the streets for a little

distance, but to no purpose. The wind blew the snow up in such heaps that it was quite impossible to follow any trail under such conditions.

With an expression of impatience Muller gave up his search and turned to go back again. He was hoping that Amster might have had better luck. It was not possible to find the goal towards which the wagon had taken its prisoner — if prisoner she was — as soon as they had hoped. Perhaps the search must be made in the direction from which she had been brought.

Muller turned back towards the city again. He walked more quickly now, but his eyes took in everything to the right and to the left of his path. Near the place where the street divided a bush waved its bare twigs in the wind. The snow which had settled upon it early in the day had been blown away by the freshening wind, and just as Muller neared the bush he saw something white fluttering from one twig. It was a handkerchief, which had probably hung heavy and lifeless when he had passed that way before. Now when the wind held it out straight, he saw it at once. He loosened it carefully from the thorny twigs. A delicate and rather unusual perfume wafted up to his face. There was more of the odour on the little cloth than is commonly used by people of good taste. And yet this handkerchief was far too fine and delicate in texture to belong to the sort of people who habitually passed along this street. It must have something to do with the mysterious carriage. It was still quite dry, and in spite of the fact that the wind had been playing with it, it had been but slightly torn. It could therefore have been in that position for a short time only. At the nearest lantern Muller saw that the monogram on the handkerchief was the same in style and initials as that on the notebook. It was the letters A. L.

CHAPTER TWO.
THE STORY OF THE NOTEBOOK

It was warm and comfortable in the little room where Muller sat. He closed the windows, lit the gas, took off his overcoat — Muller was a pedantically careful person — smoothed his hair and sat down comfortably at the table. Just as he took up the little book, the attendant brought the tea, which he proceeded at once to enjoy. He did not take up his little book again until he had lit himself a cigar. He looked at the cover of the dainty little notebook for many minutes before he opened it. It was a couple of inches long, of the usual form, and had a cover of brown leather. In the left upper corner were the letters A. L. in gold. The leaves of the book, about fifty in all, were of a fine quality of paper and covered with close writing. On the first leaves the writing was fine and delicate, calm and orderly, but later on it was irregular and uncertain, as if penned by a trembling hand under stress of terror. This change came in the leaves of the book which followed the strange and terrible title, "How I was murdered."

Before Muller began to read he felt the covers of the book carefully. In one of them there was a tiny pocket, in which he found a little piece of wall paper of a noticeable and distinctly ugly pattern. The paper had a dark blue ground with clumsy lines of gold on it. In the pocket he found also a tramway ticket, which had been crushed and then carefully smoothed out again. After looking at these papers, Muller replaced them in the cover of the notebook. The book itself was strongly perfumed with the same odour which had exhaled from the handkerchief.

The detective did not begin his reading in that part of the book which followed the mysterious title, as the commissioner had done. He began instead at the very first words.

"Ah! she is still young," he murmured, when he had read the first lines. "Young, in easy circumstances, happy and contented."

These first pages told of pleasure trips, of visits from and to good friends, of many little events of every-day life. Then came some accounts, written in pencil, of shopping expeditions to the city. Costly laces and jewels had been bought, and linen garments for children by the dozen. "She is rich, generous, and charitable," thought the detective, for the book showed that the considerable sums which had been spent here had not been for the writer herself. The laces bore the mark, "For our church"; behind the account for the linen stood the words, "For the charity school."

Muller began to feel a strong sympathy for the writer of these notices. She showed an orderly, almost pedantic, character, mingled with generosity of heart. He turned leaf after leaf until he finally came to the words, written in intentionally heavy letters, "How I was murdered."

Muller's head sank down lower over these mysterious words, and his eyes flew through the writing that followed. It was quite a different writing here. The hand that penned these words must have trembled in deadly terror. Was it terror of coming death, foreseen and not to be escaped? or was it the trembling and the terror of an overthrown brain? It was undoubtedly, in spite of the difference, the same hand that had penned the first pages of the book. A few characteristic turns of the writing were plainly to be seen in both parts of the story. But the ink was quite different also. The first pages had been written with a delicate violet ink, the later leaves were penned with a black ink of uneven quality, of the kind used by poor people who write very seldom. The words of this later portion of the book were blurred in many places, as if the writer had not been able to dry them properly before she turned the leaves. She therefore had had neither blotting paper nor sand at her disposal.

And then the weird title!

Was it written at the dictation of insanity? or did A. L. know, while she wrote it, that it was too late for any help to reach her? Did she see her doom approaching so clearly that she knew there was no escape?

Muller breathed a deep breath before he continued his reading. Later on his breath came more quickly still, and he clinched his fist several times, as if deeply moved. He was not a cold man, only thoroughly self-controlled. In his breast there lived an unquenchable hatred of all evil. It was this that awakened the talents which made him the celebrated detective he had become.

"I fear that it will be impossible for any one to save me now, but perhaps I may be avenged. Therefore I will write down here all that has happened to me since I set out on my journey." These were the first words that were written under the mysterious title. Muller had just read them when the commissioner entered.

"Will you speak to Amster; he has just returned?" he asked.

Muller rose at once. "Certainly. Did you telegraph to all the railway stations?"

"Yes," answered the commissioner, "and also to the other police stations."

"And to the hospitals? — asylums?"

"No, I did not do that." Commissioner von Mayringen blushed, a blush that was as becoming to him as was his frank acknowledgment of his mistake. He went out to remedy it at once, while Muller heard Amster's short and not particularly important report. The workingman was evidently shivering, and the detective handed him a glass of tea with a good portion of rum in it.

"Here, drink this; you are cold. Are you ill?" Amster smiled sadly. "No, I am not ill, but I was discharged to-day and am out of work now —

that's almost as bad."

"Are you married?"

"No, but I have an old mother to support."

"Leave your address with the commissioner. He may be able to find work for you; we can always use good men here. But now drink your tea." Amster drank the glass in one gulp. "Well, now we have lost the trail in both directions," said Muller calmly. "But we will find it again. You can help, as you are free now anyway. If you have the talent for that sort of thing, you may find permanent work here."

A gesture and a look from the workingman showed the detective that the former did not think very highly of such occupation. Muller laid his hand on the other's shoulder and said gravely: "You wouldn't care to take service with us? This sort of thing doesn't rate very high, I know. But I tell you that if we have our hearts in the right place, and our brains are worth anything, we are of more good to humanity than many an honest citizen who wouldn't shake hands with us. There — and now I am busy. Goodnight."

With these words Muller pushed the astonished man out of the room, shut the door, and sat down again with his little book. This is what he read:

"Wednesday — is it Wednesday? They brought me a newspaper to-day which had the date of Wednesday, the 20th of November. The ink still smells fresh, but it is so damp here, the paper may have been older. I do not know surely on what day it is that I begin to write this narrative. I do not know either whether I may not have been ill for days and weeks; I do not know what may have been the matter with me — I know only that I was unconscious, and that when I came to myself again, I was here in this gloomy room. Did any physician see me? I have seen no one until to-day except the old woman, whose name I do not know and who has so little to say. She is kind to me otherwise, but I am afraid of her hard face and of the smile with which she answers all my questions and entreaties. 'You are ill.' These are the only words that she has ever said to me, and she pointed to her forehead as she spoke them. She thinks I am insane, therefore, or pretends to think so.

"What a hoarse voice she has. She must be ill herself, for she coughs all night long. I can hear it through the wall — she sleeps in the next room. But I am not ill, that is I am not ill in the way she says. I have no fever now, my pulse is calm and regular. I can remember everything, until I took that drink of tea in the railway station. What could there have been in that tea? I suppose I should have noticed how anxious my travelling companion was to have me drink it.

"Who could the man have been? He was so polite, so fatherly in his anxiety about me. I have not seen him since then. And yet I feel that it is he who has brought me into this trap, a trap from which I may never escape alive. I will describe him. He is very tall, stout and blond, and wears a long heavy beard, which is slightly mixed with grey. On his right cheek his beard only partly hides a long scar. His eyes are hidden by large smoked glasses. His voice is low and gentle, his manners most correct — except for his giving people poison or whatever else it was in that tea.

"I did not suffer any — at least I do not remember anything except becoming unconscious. And I seem to have felt a pain like an iron ring around my head. But I am not insane, and this fear that I feel does not spring from my imagination, but from the real danger by which I am surrounded. I am very hungry, but I do not dare to eat anything except eggs, which cannot be tampered with. I tasted some soup yesterday, and it seemed to me that it had a queer taste. I will eat nothing that is at all suspicious. I will be in my full senses when my murderers come; they shall not kill me by poison at least.

"When I came to my senses again — it was the evening of the day before yesterday — I found a letter on the little table beside my bed. It was written in French, in a handwriting that I had never seen before, and there was no signature.

"This strange letter demanded of me that I should write to my guardian, calmly and clearly, to say that for reasons which I did not intend to reveal, I had taken my own life. If I did this my present place of sojourn would be exchanged for a far more agreeable one, and I would soon be quite free. But if I did not do it, I would actually be put to death. A pen, ink and paper were ready there for the answer.

"'Never,' I wrote. And then despair came over me, and I may have indeed appeared insane. The old woman came in. I entreated and implored her to tell me why this dreadful fate should have overtaken me. She remained quite indifferent and I sank back, almost fainting, on the bed. She laid a moist cloth over my face, a cloth that had a peculiar odour. I soon fell asleep. It seemed to me that there was some one else besides the woman in the room with me. Or was she talking to herself? Next morning the letter and my answer had disappeared. It was as I thought; there was some one else in my room. Some one who had come on the tramway. I found the ticket on the carpet beside my bed. I took it and put it in my notebook!!!!!

"I believe that it is Sunday to-day. It is four days now since I have been conscious. The first sound that I remember hearing was the blast of a horn. It must come from a factory very near me. The old windows in my room rattle at the sound. I hear it mornings and evenings and at noon, on week days. I did not hear it to-day, so it must be Sunday. It was Monday, the 18th of November, that I set out on my trip, and reached here in the evening — (here? I do not know where I am), that is, I set out for Vienna, and I know that I reached the Northern Railway station there in safety.

"I was cold and felt a little faint — and then he offered me the tea — and what happened after that? Where am I? The paper that they gave me may have been a day or two old or more. And to-day is Sunday — is it the first Sunday since my departure from home? I do not know. I know only this, that I set out on the 18th of November to visit my kind old guardian, and to have a last consultation with him before my coming of age. And I know also that I have fallen into the hands of some one who has an interest in my disappearance.

"There is some one in the next room with the old woman. I hear a man's voice and they are quarrelling. They are talking of me. He wants her to do something which she will not do. He commands her to go away, but she refuses. What does he mean to do? I do not want her to leave me alone. I do not hate her any more; I know that she is not bad. When I listened I heard her speaking of me as of an insane person. She really believes that I am ill. When the man went away he must have been angry. He stamped down the stairs until the steps creaked under his tread: I know it is a wooden staircase therefore.

"I am safe from him to-day, but I am really ill of fright. Am I really insane? There is one thing that I have forgotten to write down. When I first came to myself I found a bit of paper beside me on which was written, 'Beware of calling in help from outside. One scream will mean death to you.' It was written in French like the letter. Why? Was it because the old woman could not read it? She knew of the piece of paper, for she took it away from me. It frightens me that I should have forgotten to write this down. Am I really ill? If I am not yet ill, this terrible solitude will make me so.

"What a gloomy room this is, this prison of mine. And such a strange ugly wall-paper. I tore off a tiny bit of it and hid it in this little book. Some one may find it some day and may discover from it this place where I am suffering, and where I shall die, perhaps. There cannot be many who would buy such a pattern, and it must be possible to find the factory where it was made. And I will also write down here what I can see from my barred window. Far down below me there is a rusty tin roof, it looks like as if it might belong to a sort of shed. In front and to the right there are windowless walls; to the left, at a little distance, I can see a slender church spire, greenish in colour, probably covered with copper, and before the church there are two poplar trees of diffcrent heights.

"Another day has passed, a day of torturing fear! Am I really insane? I know that I see queer things. This morning I looked towards the window and I saw a parrot sitting there! I saw it quite plainly. It ruffled up its red and green feathers and stared at me. I stared back at it and suddenly it was gone. I shivered. Finally I pulled myself together and went to the window. There was no bird outside nor was there a trace of any in the snow on the window sill. Could the wind have blown away the tracks so soon, or was it really my sick brain that appeared to see this tropical bird in the midst of the snow? It is Tuesday today; from now on I will carefully count the days — the days that still remain to me.

"This morning I asked the old woman about the parrot. She only smiled and her smile made me terribly afraid. The thought that this thing which is happening to me, this thing that I took to be a crime, may be only a necessity — the thought fills me with horror! Am I in a prison? or is this the cell of an insane asylum? Am I the victim of a villain? or am I really mad? My pulse is quickening, but my memory is quite clear; I can look back over every incident in my life.

"She has just taken away my food. I asked her to bring me only eggs as I was afraid of everything else. She promised that she would do it.

"Are they looking for me? My guardian is Theodore Fellner, Cathedral Lane, 14. My own name is Asta Langen.

"They took away my travelling bag, but they did not find this little book and the tiny bottle of perfume which I had in the pocket of my dress.

And I found this old pen and a little ink in a drawer of the writing table in my room.

"Wednesday. The stranger was here again to-day. I recognised his soft voice. He spoke to the woman in the hall outside my room. I listened, but I could catch only a few words. 'To-morrow evening — I will come myself — no responsibility for you.' Were these words meant for me? Are they going to take me away? Where will they take me? Then they do not dare to kill me here? My head is burning hot. I have not dared to drink a drop of liquid for four days. I dare not take anything into which they might have put some drug or some poison.

"Who could have such an interest in my death? It cannot be because of the fortune which is to be mine when I come of age; for if I die, my father has willed it to various charitable institutions. I have no relatives, at least none who could inherit my money. I had never harmed any one; who can wish for my death?

"There is somebody with her, somebody was listening at the door. I have a feeling as if I was being watched. And yet — I examined the door, but there is no crack anywhere and the key is in the lock. Still I seem to feel a burning glance resting on me. Ah! the parrot! is this another delusion? Oh God, let it end soon! I am not yet quite insane, but all these unknown dangers around me will drive me mad. I must fight against them.

"Thursday. They brought me back my travelling bag. My attendant is uneasy. She was longer in cleaning up the room than usual to-day. She seemed to want to say something to me, and yet she did not dare to speak. Is something to happen to-day then? I did not close my eyes all night. Can one be made insane from a distance? hypnotised into it, as it were? I will not allow fear alone to make me mad. My enemy shall not find it too easy. He may kill my body, but that is all — "

These were the last words which Asta Langen had written in her notebook, the little book which was the only confidant of her terrible need. When the detective had finished reading it, he closed his eyes for a few minutes to let the impression made by the story sink into his mind.

Then he rose and put on his overcoat. He entered the commissioner's room and took up his hat and cane.

"Where are you going, Muller?" asked Herr Von Mayringen.

"To Cathedral Lane, if you will permit it."

"At this hour? it is quarter past eleven! Is there any such hurry, do you think? There is no train from any of our stations until morning. And I have already sent a policeman to watch the house. Besides, I know that Fellner is a highly respected man.

"There is many a man who is highly respected until he is found out," remarked the detective.

"And you are going to find out about Fellner?" smiled the commissioner. "And this evening, too?"

"This very evening. If he is asleep I shall wake him up. That is the best time to get at the truth about a man."

The commissioner sat down at his desk and wrote out the necessary credentials for the detective. A few moments later Muller was in the street. He left the notebook with the commissioner. It was snowing heavily, and an icy north wind was howling through the streets. Muller turned up the collar of his coat and walked on quickly. It was just striking a quarter to twelve when he reached Cathedral Lane. As he walked slowly along the moonlit side of the pavement, a man stepped out of the shadow to meet him. It was the policeman who had been sent to watch the house. Like Muller, he wore plain clothes.

"Well?" the latter asked.

"Nothing new. Mr. Fellner has been ill in bed several days, quite seriously ill, they tell me. The janitor seems very fond of him.

"Hm — we'll see what sort of a man he is. You can go back to the station now, you must be nearly frozen standing here."

Muller looked carefully at the house which

bore the number 14. It was a handsome, old-fashioned building, a true patrician mansion which looked worthy of all confidence. But Muller knew that the outside of a house has very little to do with the honesty of the people who live in it. He rang the bell carefully, as he wished no one but the janitor to hear him.

The latter did not seem at all surprised to find a stranger asking for the owner of the house at so late an hour. "You come with a telegram, I suppose? Come right up stairs then, I have orders to let you in."

These were the words with which the old janitor greeted Muller. The detective could see from this that Mr. Theodore Fellner's conscience must be perfectly clear. The expected telegram probably had something to do with the non-appearance of Asta Langen, of whose terrible fate her guardian evidently as yet knew nothing. The janitor knocked on one of the doors, which was opened in a few moments by an old woman.

"Is it the telegram?" she asked sleepily.

"Yes," said the janitor.

"No," said Muller, "but I want to speak to Mr. Fellner."

The two old people stared at him in surprise.

"To speak to him?" said the woman, and shook her head as if in doubt. "Is it about Miss Langen?"

"Yes, please wake him."

"But he is ill, and the doctor — "

"Please wake him up. I will take the responsibility."

"But who are you?" asked the janitor.

Muller smiled a little at this belated caution on the part of the old man, and answered. "I will tell Mr. Fellner who I am. But please announce me at once. It concerns the young lady." His expression was so grave that the woman waited no longer, but let him in and then disappeared through another door. The janitor stood and looked at Muller with half distrustful, half anxious glances.

"It's no good news you bring," he said after a few minutes.

"You may be right."

"Has anything happened to our dear young lady?"

"Then you know Miss Asta Langen and her family?"

"Why, of course. I was in service on the estate when all the dreadful things happened."

"What things?"

"Why the divorce — and — but you are a stranger and I shouldn't talk about these family affairs to you. You had better tell me what has happened to our young lady."

"I must tell that to your master first."

The woman came back at this moment and said to Muller, "Come with me, please. Berner, you are to stay here until the gentleman goes out again."

Muller followed her through several rooms into a large bed-chamber where he found an elderly man, very evidently ill, lying in bed.

"Who are you?" asked the sick man, raising his head from the pillow. The woman had gone out and closed the door behind her.

"My name is Muller, police detective. Here are my credentials."

Fellner glanced hastily at the paper. "Why does the police send to me?"

"It concerns your ward."

Fellner sat upright in bed now. He leaned over towards his visitor as he said, pointing to a letter on the table beside his bed, "Asta's overseer writes me from her estate that she left home on the 18th of November to visit me. She should have reached here on the evening of the 18th, and she has not arrived yet. I did not receive this letter until to-day."

"Did you expect the young lady?"

"I knew only that she would arrive sometime

before the third of December. That date is her twenty-fourth birthday and she was to celebrate it here."

"Did she not usually announce her coming to you?"

"No, she liked to surprise me. Three days ago I sent her a telegram asking her to bring certain necessary papers with her. This brought the answer from the overseer of her estate, an answer which has caused me great anxiety. Your coming makes it worse, for I fear — " The sick man broke off and turned his eyes on Muller; eyes so full of fear and grief that the detective's heart grew soft. He felt Fellner's icy hand on his as the sick man murmured: "Tell me the truth! Is Asta dead?"

The detective shrugged his shoulders. "We do not know yet. She was alive and able to send a message at half past eight this evening."

"A message? To whom?"

"To the nearest police station." Muller told the story as it had come to him.

The old man listened with an expression of such utter dazed terror that the detective dropped all suspicion of him at once.

"What a terrible riddle," stammered the sick man as the other finished the story.

"Would you answer me several questions?" asked Muller. The old gentleman answered quickly, "Any one, every one."

"Miss Langen is rich?"

"She has a fortune of over three hundred thousand guldens, and considerable land."

"Has she any relatives?"

"No," replied Fellner harshly. But a thought must have flashed through his brain for he started suddenly and murmured, "Yes, she has one relative, a step-brother."

The detective gave an exclamation of surprise.

"Why are you astonished at this?" asked Fellner.

"According to her notebook, the young lady does not seem to know of this step-brother."

"She does not know, sir. There was an ugly scandal in her family before her birth. Her father turned his first wife and their son out of his house on one and the same day. He had discovered that she was deceiving him, and also that her son, who was studying medicine at the time, had stolen money from his safe. What he had discovered about his wife made Langen doubt whether the boy was his son at all. There was a terrible scene, and the two disappeared from their home forever. The woman died soon after. The young man went to Australia. He has never been heard of since and has probably come to no good."

"Might he not possibly be here in Europe again, watching for an opportunity to make a fortune?"

Fellner's hand grasped that of his visitor. The eyes of the two men gazed steadily at each other. The old man's glance was full of sudden helpless horror, the detective's eyes shone brilliantly. Muller spoke calmly: "This is one clue. Is there no one else who could have an interest in the young lady's death?"

"No one but Egon Langen, if he bear this name by right, and if he is still alive."

"How old would he be now?"

"He must be nearly forty. It was many years before Langen married again."

"Do you know him personally?"

"Have you a picture of Miss Langen?"

Fellner rang a bell and Berner appeared. "Give this gentleman Miss Asta's picture. Take the one in the silver frame on my desk;" the old gentleman's voice was friendly but faint with fatigue. His old servant looked at him in deep anxiety. Fellner smiled weakly and nodded to the man. "Sad news, Berner! Sad news and bad news. Our poor Asta is being held a prisoner by some unknown villain who threatens her with death."

"My God, is it possible? Can't we help the poor young lady?"

"We will try to help her, or if it is — too late, we will at least avenge her. My entire fortune shall be given up for it. But bring her picture now."

Berner brought the picture of a very pretty girl with a bright intelligent face. Muller took the picture out of the frame and put it in his pocket.

"You will come again? soon? And remember, I will give ten thousand guldens to the man who saves Asta, or avenges her. Tell the police to spare no expense — I will go to headquarters myself to-morrow."

Fellner was a little surprised that Muller, although he had already taken up his hat, did not go. The sick man had seen the light flash up in the eyes of the other as he named the sum. He thought he understood this excitement, but it touched him unpleasantly and he sank back, almost frightened, in his cushions as the detective bent over him with the words "Good. Do not forget your promise, for I will save Miss Langen or avenge her. But I do not want the money for myself. It is to go to those who have been unjustly convicted and thus ruined for life. It may give the one or the other of them a better chance for the future."

"And you? what good do you get from that?" asked the old gentleman, astonished. A soft smile illumined the detective's plain features and he answered gently, "I know then that there will be some poor fellow who will have an easier time of it than I have had."

He nodded to Fellner, who had already grasped his hand and pressed it hard. A tear ran down his grey beard, and long after Muller had gone the old gentleman lay pondering over his last words.

Berner led the visitor to the door. As he was opening it, Muller asked: "Has Egon Langen a bad scar on his right cheek?"

Berner's eyes looked his astonishment. How did the stranger know this? And how did he come to mention this forgotten name.

"Yes, he has, but how did you know it?" he murmured in surprise. He received no answer, for Muller was already walking quickly down the street. The old man stared after him for some few minutes, then suddenly his knees began to tremble. He closed the door with difficulty, and sank down on a bench beside it. The wind had blown out the light of his lantern; Berner was sitting in the dark without knowing it, for a sudden terrible light had burst upon his soul, burst upon it so sharply that he hid his eyes with his hands, and his old lips murmured, "Horrible! Horrible! The brother against the sister."

The next morning was clear and bright. Muller was up early, for he had taken but a few hours sleep in one of the rooms of the station, before he set out into the cold winter morning. At the next corner he found Amster waiting for him. "What are you doing here?" he asked in astonishment.

"I have been thinking over what you said to me yesterday. Your profession is as good and perhaps better than many another."

"And you come out here so early to tell me that?"

Amster smiled. "I have something else to say."

"Well?"

"The commissioner asked me yesterday if I knew of a church in the city that had a slender spire with a green top and two poplars in front of it."

Muller looked his interest.

"I thought it might possibly be the Convent Church of the Grey Sisters, but I wasn't quite sure, so I went there an hour ago. It's all right, just as I thought. And I suppose it has something to do with the case of last night, so I thought I had better report at once. I was on my way to the station."

"That will do very well. You have saved us much time and you have shown that you are eminently fitted for this business."

"If you really will try me, then — "

"We'll see. You can begin on this. Come to

the church with me now." Muller was no talker, particularly not when, as now, his brain was busy on a problem.

The two men walked on quickly. In about half an hour they found themselves in a little square in the middle of which stood an old church. In front of the church, like giant sentinels, stood a pair of tall poplars. One of them looked sickly and was a good deal shorter than its neighbour. Muller nodded as if content.

"Is this the church the commissioner was talking about?" queried Amster.

"It is," was the answer. Muller walked on toward a little house built up against the church, which was evidently the dwelling of the sexton.

The detective introduced himself to this official, who did not look over-intelligent, as a stranger in the city who had been told that the view from the tower of the church was particularly interesting. A bright silver piece banished all distrust from the soul of the worthy man. With great friendliness he inquired when the gentlemen would like to ascend the tower. "At once," was the answer.

The sexton took a bunch of keys and told the strangers to follow him. A few moments later Muller and his companion stood in the tiny belfry room of the slender spire. The fat sexton, to his own great satisfaction, had yielded to their request not to undertake the steep ascent. The cloudless sky lay crystal clear over the still sleeping city and the wide spread snow-covered fields which lay close at hand, beyond the church. On the one side were gardens and the low rambling buildings of the convent, and on the other were huddled high-piled dwellings of poverty.

Muller looked out of each of the four windows in turn. He spent some time at each window, but evidently without discovering what he looked for, for he shook his head in discontent. But when he went once more to the opening in the East, into which the sun was just beginning to pour its light, something seemed to attract his attention. He called Amster and pointed from the window. "Your eyes are younger than mine, lend them to me. What do you see over there to the right, below the tall factory chimney?" Muller's voice was calm, but there was something in his manner that revealed excitement. Amster caught the infection without knowing why. He looked sharply in the direction towards which Muller pointed, and began: "There is a tall house near the chimney, to the right of it, one wall touching it. The house is crowded in between other newer buildings, and looks to be very old and of a much better sort than its neighbours. The other houses are plain stone, but this house has carvings and statues on it, which are white with snow. But the house is in bad condition, one can see cracks in the wall."

"And its windows?"

"I cannot see them. They must be on the other side of the house, towards the courtyard which seems to be hemmed in by the blank walls of the other houses."

"And at the front of the house?"

"There is a low wall in front which shuts off the courtyard from a narrow, ill-kept street."

"Yes, I see it myself now. The street is bordered mainly by gardens and vacant lots."

"Yes, sir, that is it." Muller nodded as if satisfied. Amster looked at him in surprise, still more surprised, however, at the excitement he felt himself. He did not understand it, but Muller understood it. He knew that he had found in Amster a talent akin to his own, one of those natures who once having taken up a trail cannot rest until they reach their goal. He looked for a few moments in satisfaction at the assistant he had found by such chance, then he turned and hastened down the stairs again.

"We're going to that house?" asked Amster when they were down in the street. Muller nodded.

Without hesitation the two men made their way through a tangle of dingy, uninteresting alleys, between modern tenements, until about ten minutes later they stood before an old three-storied building, which had a frontage of four windows on the street. "This is our place," said the detective, looking up at the tall, handsome gateway and the rococo carvings that ornamented the front of this decaying dwelling. It was very evidently of a different age and class from those about it.

Muller had already raised his hand to pull the bell, when he stopped and let it sink again. His eye caught sight of a placard pasted up on the wall of the next house, and already half torn off by the wind. The detective walked over, and raising the placard with his cane, read the words on it. "That's right," he said to himself. Amster gave a look on the paper. But he could not connect the contents of the notice with the case of the kidnapped lady, and he shook his head in surprise when Muller turned to him with the words: "The lady we are looking for is not insane." On the paper was announced in large letters that a reward would be offered to the finder of a red and green parrot which had escaped from a neighbouring house.

Muller rang the bell and they had to wait some few minutes before the door opened with great creakings, and the towsled head of an old woman peered out.

"What do you want?" she asked hoarsely, with distrustful looks.

"Let us in, and then give us the keys of the upstairs rooms." Muller's voice was friendly, but the woman grew perceptibly paler.

"Who are you?" she stammered. Muller threw back his overcoat and showed her his badge. "But there is nobody here, the house is quite empty."

"There were a lady and gentleman here last evening." The woman threw a frightened look at Muller, then she said hesitatingly: "The lady was insane and has been taken to an asylum."

"That is what the man told you. He is a criminal and the police are looking for him."

"Come with me," murmured the woman. She seemed to understand that further resistance was useless. She carefully locked the outside door. Amster remained down stairs in the corridor, while Muller followed the old woman up the stairs. The staircase to the third story was made of wood. The house was evidently very old, with low ceilings and many dark corners.

The woman led Muller into the room in which she had cared for the strange lady at the order of the latter's "husband." He had told her that it was only until he could take the lady to an asylum. One look at the wall paper, a glance out of the window, and Muller knew that this was where Asta Langen had been imprisoned. He sat down on a chair and looked at the woman, who stood frightened before him.

"Do you know where they have taken the lady?"

"No, sir.

"Do you know the gentleman's name?"

"No, sir.

"You did not send the lady's name to the authorities?" *

"No, sir."

(* Any stranger taking rooms in a hotel or lodging house must be registered with the police authorities by the proprietor of the house within forty-eight hours of arrival.)

"Were you not afraid you would get into trouble?"

"The gentleman paid me well, and I did not think that he meant anything bad, and — and — "

"And you did not think that it would be found out?" said Muller sternly.

"I took good care of the lady."

"Yes, we know that."

"Did she escape from her husband?"

"He was not her husband. But now tell me all you know about these people; the more truthful you are the better it will be for you."

The old woman was so frightened that she could scarcely find strength to talk. When she finally got control of herself again she began: "He came here on the first of November and rented this room for himself. But he was here only twice before he brought the lady and left her alone here. She was very ill when he brought her here — so ill that he had to carry her upstairs. I wanted to go for a doctor, but he said he was a doctor himself, and that he could take care of his wife, who often had such attacks. He gave me some medicine for her after I had put her to bed. I gave her the drops, but it was a long while before she came to herself again.

"Then he told me that she had lost her mind, and that she believed everybody was trying to harm her. She was so bad that he was taking her to an asylum. But he hadn't found quite the right place yet, and wanted me to keep her here until he knew where he could take her. Once he left a revolver here by mistake. But I hid it so the lady wouldn't see it, and gave it to the gentleman the next time he came. He was angry at that, though I couldn't see why, and said I shouldn't have touched it."

The woman had told her story with much hesitation, and stopped altogether at this point. She had evidently suddenly realised that the lady was not insane, but only in great despair, and that people in such a state will often seek death, particularly if any weapon is left conveniently within their reach.

"What did this gentleman look like?" asked Muller, to start her talking again. She described her tenant as very tall and stout with a long beard slightly mixed with grey. She had never seen his eyes, for he wore smoked glasses.

"Did you notice anything peculiar about his face?"

"No, nothing except that his beard was ver heavy and almost covered his face."

"Could you see his cheeks at all?"

"No, or else I didn't notice."

"Did he leave nothing that might enable us to find him?"

"No, sir, nothing. Or yes, perhaps, but I don't suppose that will be any good."

"What was it? What do you mean?"

"It gave him a good deal of trouble to get the lady into the wagon, because she had fainted again. He lost his glove in doing it. I have it down stairs in my room, for I sleep down stairs again since the lady has gone."

Muller had risen from his chair and walked over to the old writing desk which stood beside one window. There were several sheets of ordinary brown paper on it and sharp pointed pencil and also something not usually found on writing desks, a piece of bread from which some of the inside had been taken. "Everything as I expected it," he said to himself. "The young lady made up the package in the last few moments that she was left alone here."

49

He turned again to the old woman and commanded her to lead him down stairs. "What sort of a carriage was it in which they took the lady away?" he asked as they went down.

"A closed coupe."

"Did you see the number?"

"No, sir. But the carriage was very shabby and so was the driver."

"Was he an old man?"

"He was about forty years old, but he looked like a man who drank. He had a light-coloured overcoat on."

"Good. Is this your room?"

"Yes, sir."

They were now in the lower corridor, where they found Amster walking up and down. The woman opened the door of the little room, and took a glove from a cupboard. Muller put it in his pocket and told the woman not to leave the house for anything, as she might be sent for to come to the police station at any moment. Then he went out into the street with Amster. When they were outside in the sunlight, he looked at the glove. It was a remarkably small size, made for a man with a slender, delicate hand, not at all in accordance with the large stout body of the man described by the landlady. Muller put his hand into the glove and found something pushed up into the middle finger. He took it out and found that it was a crumpled tramway ticket.

"Look out for a shabby old closed coupe, with a driver about forty years old who looks like a drunkard and wears a light overcoat. If you find such a cab, engage it and drive in it to the nearest police station. Tell them there to hold the man until further notice. If the cab is not free, at least take his number. And one thing more, but you will know that yourself, — the cab we are looking for will have new glass in the right-hand window." Thus Muller spoke to his companion as he put the glove into his pocket and unfolded the tramway ticket. Amster understood that they had found the starting point of the drive of the night before.

"I will go to all coupe stands," he said eagerly.

"Yes, but we may be able to find it quicker than that." Muller took the little notebook, which he was now carrying in his pocket, and took from it the tramway ticket which was in the cover. He compared it with the one he had just found. They were both marked for the same hour of the day and for the same ride.

"Did the man use them?" asked Amster. The detective nodded. "How can they help us?"

"Somewhere on this stretch of the street railroad you will probably find the stand of the cab we are looking for. The man who hired it evidently arrived on the 6:30 train at the West Station — I have reason to believe that he does not live here, — and then took the street car to this corner. The last ticket is marked for yesterday. In the car he probably made his plans to hire a cab. So you had better stay along the line of the car tracks. You will find me in room seven, Police Headquarters, at noon to-day. The authorities have already taken up the case. You may have something to tell us then. Good luck to you."

Muller hurried on, after he had taken a quick breakfast in a little cafe. He went at once to headquarters, made his report there and then drove to Fellner's house. The latter was awaiting him with great impatience. There the detective gathered much valuable information about the first marriage of Asta Langen's long-dead father. It was old Berner who could tell him the most about these long-vanished days.

When he reached his office at headquarters again, he found telegrams in great number awaiting him. They were from all the hospitals and insane asylums in the entire district. But in none of them had there been a patient fitting the description of the vanished girl. Neither the commissioner nor Muller was surprised at this negative result. They were also not surprised at all that the other branches of the police department had been able to discover so little about the disappearance of the young lady. They were aware that they had to deal with a criminal of great ability who would be careful not to fall into the usual slips made by his kind.

There was no news from the cab either, although several detectives were out looking for it. It was almost nightfall when Amster ran breathlessly into room number seven. "I have him! he's waiting outside across the way!" This was Amster's report.

Muller threw on his coat hastily. "You didn't pay him, did you? On a cold day like this the drivers don't like to wait long in any one place."

"No danger. I haven't money enough for that," replied Amster with a sad smile. Muller did not hear him as he was already outside. But the commissioner with whom he had been talking and to whom Muller had already spoken of his voluntary assistant, entered into a conversation with Amster, and said to him finally: "I will take it upon myself to guarantee your future, if you are ready to enter the secret service under Muller's orders. If you wish to do this you can stay right on now, for I think we will need you in this case."

Amster bowed in agreement. His life had been troubled, his reputation darkened by no fault of his own, and the work he was doing now had awakened, an interest and an ability that he did not know he possessed. He was more than glad to accept the offer made by the official.

Muller was already across the street and had

laid his hand upon the door of the cab when the driver turned to him and said crossly, "Some one else has ordered me. But I am not going to wait in this cold, get in if you want to."

"All right. Now tell me first where you drove to last evening with the sick lady and her companion?" The man looked astonished but found his tongue again in a moment. "And who are you?" he asked calmly.

"We will tell you that upstairs in the police station," answered Muller equally calmly, and ordered the man to drive through the gateway into the inner courtyard. He himself got into the wagon, and in the course of the short drive he had made a discovery. He had found a tiny glass stopper, such as is used in perfume bottles. He could understand from this why the odour of perfume which had now become familiar to him was still so strong inside the old cab. Also why it was so strong on the delicate handkerchief. Asta Langen had taken the stopper from the bottle in her pocket, so as to leave a trail of odour behind her.

CHAPTER THREE.
THE LONELY COTTAGE

Fifteen minutes after the driver had made his report to Commissioner Von Mayringen, the latter with Amster entered another cab. A well-armed policeman mounted the box of this second vehicle. "Follow that cab ahead," the commissioner told his driver. The second cab followed the one-horse coupe in which Muller was seated. They drove first to No. 14 Cathedral Lane, where Muller told Berner to come with him. He found Mr. Fellner ready to go also, and it was with great difficulty that he could dissuade the invalid, who was greatly fatigued by his morning visit to the police station, from joining them.

The carriages then drove off more quickly than before. It was now quite dark, a gloomy stormy winter evening. Muller had taken his place on the box of his cab and sat peering out into the darkness. In spite of the sharp wind and the ice that blew against his face the detective could see that they were going out from the more closely built up portions of the city, and were now in new streets with half-finished houses. Soon they passed even these and were outside of the city. The way was lonely and dreary, bordered by wooden fences on both sides. Muller looked sharply to right and to left.

"You should have become alarmed here," he said to the driver, pointing to one part of the fence.

"Why?" asked the man.

"Because this is where the window was broken."

"I didn't know that — until I got home."

"H'm; you must have been nicely drunk."

The driver murmured something in his beard.

"Stop here, this is your turn, down that street," Muller said a few moments later, as the driver turned the other way.

"How do you know that?" asked the man, surprised.

"None of your business."

"This street will take us there just the same."

"Probably, but I prefer to go the way you went yesterday."

"Very well, it's all the same to me." They were silent again, only the wind roared around them, and somewhere in the distance a fog horn moaned.

It was now six o'clock. The snow threw out a mild light which could not brighten the deep darkness around them. About half an hour later the first cab halted. "There's the house up there. Shall I drive to the garden gate?"

"No, stop here." Muller was already on the ground. "Are there any dogs here?" he asked.

"I didn't hear any yesterday."

"That's of no value. You didn't seem to hear much of anything yesterday." Muller opened the door of the cab and helped Berner out. The old man was trembling. "That was a dreadful drive!" he stammered.

"I hope you will be happier on the drive back," said the detective and added, "You stay here with the commissioner now."

The latter had already left his cab with his companion. His sharp eyes glanced over the heavily shaded garden and the little house in its midst. A little light shone from two windows of the first story. The men's eyes looked toward them, then the detective and Amster walked toward a high picket fence which closed the garden on the side nearest its neighbours. They shook the various pickets without much caution, for the wind made noise enough to kill any other sound. Amster called to Muller, he had found a loose picket, and his strong young arms had torn it out easily. Muller motioned to the other three to join them. A moment later they were all in the garden, walking carefully toward the house.

The door was closed but there were no bars at the windows of the ground floor. Amster looked inquiringly at the commissioner and the latter nodded and said, "All right, go ahead."

The next minute Amster had broken in through one pane of the window and turned the latch. The inner window was broken already so that it was not difficult for him to open it without any further noise. He disappeared into the dark room within. In a few seconds they heard a key turn in the door and it opened gently. The men entered, all except the policeman, who remained outside. The blind of his lantern was slightly opened, and he had his revolver ready in his hand.

Muller had opened his lantern also, and they saw that they were in a prettily furnished corridor from which the staircase and one door led out.

The four men tiptoed up the stairway and the commissioner stepped to the first of the two doors which opened onto the upper corridor. He turned the key which was in the lock, and opened the door, but they found themselves in a room as dark as was the corridor. From somewhere, however, a ray of light fell into the blackness. The official stepped into the room, pulling Berner in after him. The poor old man was in a state of trembling excitement when he found himself in the house where his beloved young lady might already be a corpse. One step more and a smothered cry broke from his lips. The commissioner had opened the door of an adjoining room, which was lighted and handsomely furnished. Only the heavy iron bars across the closed windows showed that the young lady who sat leaning back wearily in an arm-chair was a prisoner.

She looked up as they entered. The expression of utter despair and deep weariness which had rested on her pale face changed to a look of terror; then she saw that it was not her would-be murderer who was entering, but those who came to rescue. A bright flush illumined her cheeks and her eyes gleamed. But the change was too sudden for her tortured soul. She rose from her chair, then sank fainting to the floor.

Berner threw himself on his knees beside her, sobbing out, "She is dying! She is dying!"

Muller turned on the instant, for he had heard the door on the other side of the hall open, and a tall slender man with a smooth face and a deep scar on his right cheek stood on the threshold looking at them in dazed surprise. For an instant only had he lost his control. The next second he was in his room again, slamming the door behind him. But it was too late. Amster's foot was already in the crack of the door and he pushed it open to let Muller enter. "Well done," cried the latter, and then he turned to the man in the room. "Here, stop that. I can fire twice before you get the window open."

The man turned and walked slowly to the centre of the room, sinking down into an arm-chair that stood beside the desk. Neither Amster nor Muller turned their eyes from him for a moment, ready for any attempt on his part to escape. But the detective had already seen something that told him that Langen was not thinking of flight. When he turned to the desk, Muller had seen his eyes glisten while a scornful smile parted his thin, lips. A second later he had let his handkerchief fall, apparently carelessly, upon the desk. But in this short space of time the detective's sharp eyes had seen a tiny bottle upon which was a black label with a grinning skull. Muller could not see whether the bottle was full or empty, but now he knew that it must hold sufficient poison to enable the captured criminal to escape open disgrace. Knowing this, Muller looked with admiration at the calmness of the villain, whose intelligent eyes were turned towards him in evident curiosity.

"Who are you and who else is here with you?" asked the man calmly.

"I am Muller of the Secret Service," replied his visitor and added, "You must put up with us for the time being, Mr. Egon Langen. The police commissioner is occupied with your step-sister, whom you were about to murder."

Langen put his hand to his cheek, looking at Muller between his lashes as he said, "To murder? Who can prove that?"

"We have all the proofs we need."

"I will acknowledge only that I wanted Asta to disappear."

Muller smiled. "What good would that have done you? You wanted her entire fortune, did you not? But that could have come to you only after thirty years, and you are not likely to have waited that long. Your plan was to murder your step-sister, even if you could not get a letter from her telling of her intention to commit suicide."

Langen rose suddenly, but controlled himself again and sank back easily in his chair. "Then the old woman has been talking?" he asked.

Muller shook his head. "We knew it through Miss Langen herself."

"She has spoken to no one for over ten days."

"But you let her throw her notebook out of the window of the cab."

"Ah — "

"There, you see, you should not have let that happen."

Drops of perspiration stood out on Langen's forehead. Until now, perhaps, he had had some possible hope of escape. It was useless now, he knew.

As calmly as he had spoken thus far Muller continued. "For twenty years I have been study-ing the hearts of criminals like yourself. But there are things I do not understand about this case and it interests me very much."

Langen had wiped the drops from his forehead and he now turned on Muller a face that seemed made of bronze. There was but one expression on it, that of cold scorn.

"I feel greatly flattered, sir, to think that I can offer a problem to one of your experience," Langen began. His voice, which had been slightly veiled before, was now quite clear. "Ask me all you like. I will answer you."

Muller began: "Why did you wait so long before committing the murder? and why did you drag your victim from place to place when you could have killed her easily in the compartment of the railway train?"

"The windows of the compartment were open, my honoured friend, and it was a fine warm evening for the season, because of which the windows in the other compartment were also open. There was nothing else I could do at that time then, except to offer Asta a cup of tea when she felt a little faint upon leaving the train. I am a physician and I know how to use the right drugs at the right time. When Asta had taken the tea, she knew nothing more until she woke up a day later in a room in the city."

"And the piece of paper with the threat on it? and the revolver you left so handy for her? oh, but I forgot, the old woman took the weapon away before the lady could use it in her despair," said Muller.

"Quite right. I see you know every detail."

"But why didn't you complete your crime in the room in the old house?" persisted Muller.

"Because I lost my false beard one day upon the staircase, and I feared the old woman might have seen my face enough to recognise me again. I thought it better to look for another place."

"And then you found this house."

"Yes, but several days later."

"And you hired it in the name of Miss Asta Langen? Who would then have been found dead here several days after you had entered the house?"

"Several days, several weeks perhaps. I preferred to wait until the woman who rented the house had read in the papers that Asta Langen had disappeared and was being sought for. Somebody would have found her here, and her identity would have easily been established, for I knew that she had some important family documents with her."

Muller was silent a moment, with an expression of deep pity on his face. Then he continued: "Yes, someone would have found her, and her suicide would have been a dark mystery, unless, of course, malicious tongues would have found ugly reasons enough why a beautiful young lady should hide herself in a lonely cottage to take her own life."

Muller had spoken as if to himself. Egon

Langen's lips, parted in a smile so evil that Amster clenched his fists.

"And you would not have regretted this ruining the reputation as well as taking the life of an innocent girl?" asked the detective low and tense "No, for I hated her."

"You hated her because she was rich and innocent. She was very charitable and would gladly have helped you if you were in need. Beside this, you were entitled to a portion of your father's estate. It is almost thirty thousand guldens, as Mr. Fellner tells me. Why did you not take that?"

"Fellner did not know that I had already received twenty thousand of this when my father turned me out. He probably would have heard of it later, for Berner was the witness. I did not care for the remaining ten thousand because I would have the entire fortune after Asta's death. I would have seen the official notice and the call for heirs in Australia, and would have written from there, announcing that I was still alive. If you had come several days later I should have been a rich man within a year."

His clenched fist resting on his knee, the rascal stared out ahead of him when he ended his shameless confession. In his rage and disappointment he had not noticed that Muller's hand dropped gently to the desk and softly took a little bottle from under the handkerchief. Langen came out of his dark thoughts only when Muller's voice broke the silence. "But you miscalculated, if you expected to inherit from your sister. She is still a minor and your father's will would have given you only ten thousand guldens.

"But you forget that Asta will be twenty-four on the third of December."

"Ah, then you would have kept her alive until then."

"You understand quickly," said Langen with a mocking smile.

"But she disappeared on the eighteenth of November. How could you prove that she died after her birthday, therefore in full possession of her fortune and without leaving any will?"

"That is very simple. I buy several newspapers every day. I would have taken them up to the fourth and fifth of December and left them here with the body."

"You are more clever even than I thought," said the detective dryly as he heard the commissioner's steps behind him. Muller put a whistle to his lips and its shrill tone ran through the house, calling up the policeman who stood by the door.

Egon Langen's face was grey with pallor, his features were distorted, and yet there was the ghost of a smile on his lips as he saw his captors enter the door. He put his hand out, raised his handkerchief hastily and then a wild scream echoed through the room, a scream that ended in a ghastly groan.

"I have taken your bottle, you might as well give yourself up quietly," said Muller calmly, holding his revolver near Langen's face. The prisoner threw himself at the detective but was caught and overpowered by Amster and the policeman.

A quarter of an hour later the cabs drove back toward the city. Inside one cowered Egon Langen, watched by the policeman and Amster. Berner was on the box beside the driver, telling the now interested man the story of what had happened to his dear young lady. In the other cab sat Asta Langen with Kurt von Mayringen and Muller.

"Do you feel better now?" asked the young commissioner in sincere sympathy that was mingled with admiration for the delicate beauty of the girl beside him, an admiration heightened by her romantic story and marvelous escape.

Asta nodded and answered gently: "I feel as if some terrible weight were lifted from my heart and brain. But I doubt if I will ever forget these horrible days, when I had already come to accept it as a fact that — that I was to be murdered."

"This is the man to whom you owe your escape," said the commissioner, laying his hand on Muller's knee. Asta did not speak, but she reached out in the darkness of the cab, caught Muller's hand and would have raised it to her lips, had not the little man drawn it away hastily. "It was only my duty, dear young lady," he said. "A duty that is not onerous when it means the rescue of innocence and the preventing of crime. It is not always so, unfortunately — nor am I always so fortunate as in this case."

This indeed is what Muller calls a "case with a happy ending," for scarcely a year later, to his own great embarrassment, he found himself the most honoured guest, and a centre of attraction equally with the bridal couple, at the marriage of Kurt von Mayringen and Asta Langen. Muller asserts, however, that he is not a success in society, and that he would rather unravel fifty difficult cases than again be the "lion" at a fashionable function.